D0708253

# Usborne
# Illustrated
# Classics

### The Secret Garden
### & other stories

# Usborne
# Illustrated
# Classics

The Secret Garden
& other stories TO

# Contents

# The Railway Children

# E. Nesbit (1858-1924)

Edith Nesbit wrote a hundred years ago, when most people rode by horse, not car, and television hadn't been invented. Her stories are full of excitement, adventure and magic. *The Railway Children*, first published in 1906, is one of her most famous books. It has been adapted for television four times and has twice been made into a film.

# Chapter 1
# Change

It all began at Peter's birthday party. The servants were just bringing out the birthday cake, when the doorbell clanged sharply.

"Oh dear!" exclaimed Father. "Who can that be? Start without me, everyone. I'll be back in a minute."

Peering into the hallway, Peter saw Father leading two men into his study.

"Who are they, Mother?" asked his sister, Phyllis.

"I don't know," said
Mother, frowning.
"Stay here. I'm going
to find out."

Mother disappeared into the study for ages.
"What's going on?" asked Phyllis.
"We'll just have to wait and see," replied
Bobbie, the eldest.

Mother emerged just as the front door slammed shut. Bobbie saw a carriage and horses driving rapidly away into the night. Mother's face was icy white and her eyes glittered with tears.

"Where's Father?" demanded Peter, running into the empty study.

"He's gone away." Mother was shaking now. Bobbie reached for her hand and held it tight.

"But he hasn't even packed his clothes," said Phyllis.

"He had to go quickly – on business," Mother replied.

"Was it to do with the Government?" asked Peter. Father worked in a Government office.

"Yes. Don't ask me questions, darlings. I can't tell you anything. Please just go to bed."

Upstairs, the children tried endlessly to work out where Father had gone. The next few days were just as strange.

All the maids left. Then a FOR SALE sign went up outside the house. The beautiful furniture was sold and meals now consisted of plain, cheap food. Mother was hardly ever at home.

"What's happening?" asked Peter, finally.
"Please tell us."

"We've got to play at being poor for a bit,"
Mother replied. "We're going to leave London,
and live far away in the countryside."

"Father is going to be away for some time,"
she went on. "But everything will come right in
the end, I promise."

# Chapter 2
# A coal thief

After a long, long journey, they arrived at the new house, late at night.

Mother rushed around, digging sheets out of suitcases.

The next day, Bobbie, Peter and Phyllis woke early to explore. They raced outside until they came to a red-brick bridge.

Suddenly there was a shriek and a snort and a train shot out from under it.

"It's exactly like a dragon," Peter shouted above the noise. "Did you feel the hot air from its breath?"

"Perhaps it's going to London," Phyllis yelled.

"Father might still be there," shrieked Bobbie. "If it's a magic dragon, it'll send our love to Father. Let's wave."

They pulled out their handkerchiefs and waved them in the breeze. Out of a first class carriage window a hand waved back. It was an old gentleman's hand, holding a newspaper.

After that, the children waved every day, rain or shine, at the old gentleman on the 9:15 train to London.

The weather grew colder. Mother sat in her icy bedroom wrapped in shawls, writing stories to earn money for them all.

Bobbie, Peter and Phyllis didn't notice the cold much. They were too busy playing. But one morning, it snowed so much they had to stay inside.

"Please let me light a fire, Mother," begged Bobbie. "We're all freezing."

"Not until tonight, I'm afraid. We can't afford to burn coal all day. Put on more clothes if you're chilly."

Peter was furious. "I'm the man in this family now," he stormed. "And I think we ought to be warm."

Over the next few days Peter began to disappear without saying where he was going.

"I can't understand it," Mother said soon after. "The coal never seems to run out."

"Let's follow Pete," Bobbie whispered to Phyllis. "I'm sure he's up to something."

They trailed him all the way to the station, and watched him pile a cart with coal from a huge heap.

Then suddenly, Peter screamed.

A hand had shot out of the
darkness and grabbed
him by the shoulder.

It was Mr. Perks, the station master. "Don't you know stealing is wrong?" he shouted.

"Wasn't stealing. I was mining for treasure," sulked Peter.

"That treasure belongs to the railway, young man, not you."

"He shouldn't have done it, Mr. Perks," said Bobbie, shocked. "But he was only trying to help Mother. He's really sorry, aren't you, Pete?" She gave him a kick and Peter muttered an apology.

"Accepted," said Perks. "But don't do it again."

"I hate being poor," grumbled Peter, kicking the cobbles on their way home. "And Mother deserves better than this."

Soon after, Mother got very sick. Bobbie didn't know how they were going to pay for her medicines, until she had a brilliant idea.

She wrote a letter to the old gentleman on the 9:15 train to London and asked Mr. Perks to give it to him.

Dear Mr. (we don't know your name),

Mother is sick and we can't afford the things the doctor says she needs. This is the list:

Medicine    Port Wine

Fruit       Soda water

I don't know who else to ask. Father will pay you back when he comes home, or I will when I grow up.

Bobbie

P. S. Please give them to Mr. Perks, the station master, and Pete will fetch them.

The very next day, a huge hamper appeared, filled with medicines, as well as red roses, chocolates and lavender perfume. A week later, Bobbie, Peter and Phyllis made a banner and waved it at the 9:15 train. It said:

THANK YOU!
SHE IS MUCH BETTER!

But Mother was furious when she found out. "You must never ask strangers for things," she raged.

Bobbie was nearly in tears. "I didn't mean to be naughty."

"I know, my darling," said Mother. "But you mustn't tell everyone we're poor. We have enough to live on – just. Now we won't say any more about it."

# Chapter 3
## Red for danger

They all felt miserable for upsetting
Mother. "I know what will cheer us up!"
said Bobbie. "We can ask Mr. Perks for the
magazines people leave on trains. They'd be
fun to read."

"Let's climb down the cliff and walk along the track to the station," suggested Peter. "We've never gone that way before."

"I don't want to. It doesn't look safe." Phyllis sounded frightened.

"Baby! Scaredy-cat!" teased Peter.

"It's all right, Phil," Bobbie comforted her. "The cliff isn't that steep."

"Two against one," crowed Peter. "Come on, Phil, you'll enjoy it."

Slowly Phyllis followed her brother and sister, muttering, "I still don't want to..."

They scrambled down the cliff. Phyllis tumbled down the last bit where the steps had crumbled away, and tore her dress.

Now her red petticoat flapped through the tear as she walked.

"There!" she announced. "I told you this would be horrible, and it is!"

"No, it isn't," disagreed Peter.

"What's that noise?" asked Bobbie suddenly. A strange sound, like far off thunder, began and stopped. Then it started again, getting louder and more rumbling.

"Look at that tree!" cried Peter. The tree was moving, not like a normal tree when the wind blows, but all in one piece.

All the trees on the bank seemed to be slowly sliding downhill, like a marching army.

Suddenly, rocks, trees, grasses, bushes and earth gathered speed in a deafening roar and collapsed in a heap on the railway track.

"I don't like it!" shrieked Phyllis. "It's much too magic for me!"

"It's all coming down," said Peter in a shaky voice. Then he cried out, "Oh!"

The others looked at him. "The 11:29 train! It'll be along any minute. There'll be a terrible accident."

"Can we run to the station and tell them?" Bobbie began.

"No time. We need to warn the driver somehow. What can we do?"

"Our red petticoats!" Bobbie exclaimed. "Red for danger! We'll tear them up and use them as flags."

"We can't rip our clothes!" Phyllis objected. "What will Mother say?"

"She won't mind." Bobbie was undoing her petticoat as she spoke. "Don't you see, Phil, if we don't stop the train in time, people might be killed?"

They quickly snapped thin branches off the nearby trees, tore up the petticoats and made them into flags.

"Two each. Wave one in each hand, and stand on the track so the train can see us," Peter directed. "Then jump out of the way."

Phyllis was gasping with fright. "It's dangerous! I don't like it!"

"Think of saving the train," Bobbie implored. "That's what matters most!"

"It's coming," called Peter, though his voice was instantly wiped out in a whirlwind of sound.

As the roaring train thundered nearer and nearer, Bobbie waved her flags furiously. She was sure it was no good, that the train would never see them in time...

"MOVE!" shouted Peter, as the train's steam surrounded them in a cloud of white. But Bobbie couldn't. She had to make it stop.

With a judder and squeal of brakes the train shuddered to a halt and the driver jumped out. "What's going on?"

Peter and Phyllis showed him the landslide. But not Bobbie. She had fainted and lay on the track, white and quiet as a fallen statue, still gripping her petticoat flags.

The driver picked her up and put her in one of the first class carriages. Peter and Phyllis were worried, until finally Bobbie began to cry.

"You children saved lives today," said the driver. "I expect the Railway Company will give you a reward."

"Just like real heroes and heroines," breathed Phyllis.

# Chapter 4
## The terrible secret

The Railway Company did want to reward the
children. There was a ceremony at the station,
with a brass band, decorations and cake.

46

All the passengers who had been on the train were there, as well as the Railway Director, the train driver, Mr. Perks, and best of all, their own old gentleman.

The Railway Director made a speech praising the children, which they found very embarrassing, and gave them each a gold watch.

When it was all over, the old gentleman shook their hands.

"Oh do come back for tea," said Phyllis.

They climbed up the hill together. Bobbie carried the magazines Mr. Perks had collected for her. He'd made a package of them, wrapped in an old sheet of newspaper.

Back home, Mother, Phyllis and Peter chatted with the old gentleman.

Bobbie went into her room, to sort through the magazines. She undid the newspaper wrapping and idly looked at the print. Then she stared.

Her feet went icy cold and her face burned. When she had read it all, she drew a long, uneven breath.

"So now I know," she thought. It was a report of a spy trial, with a photograph of the accused. It was a photograph of Father. Underneath it said: GUILTY. And then: FIVE YEARS IN JAIL.

Bobbie scrunched up the paper. "Oh Daddy," she whispered. "You never did it."

Time passed. The old gentleman left and it grew dark outside. Supper was ready, but Bobbie couldn't join the others.

Mother came to find her.

"What's the matter?" she asked.

Bobbie held out the paper. "Tell me about it," she begged.

Mother told her how Father had been arrested for being a spy. Papers had been found in his desk that proved he had sold his country's secrets to enemies.

"Didn't they know he'd never do such a thing?" Bobbie asked.

"There was a man in his office he never quite trusted," Mother replied. "I think he planted those papers on Father."

"Why didn't you tell the lawyers that?" Bobbie wanted to know.

"Do you think I didn't try everything?" Mother demanded. "We just have to be patient and wait for him to come back to us."

"Why didn't you tell us?"

"Are you going to tell the others now you know?"

"No," said Bobbie.

"Why?"

Bobbie thought hard. "Because... it would only upset them."

"Exactly," said her mother. "But now you've found out, we must help each other to be brave."

They went in to supper together, and though Bobbie's eyes were still red with tears, Peter and Phyllis never guessed why.

# Chapter 5
# The man in the train

The long, cold winter blossomed into spring, and then summer. Bobbie couldn't bear the way time passed with nothing happening.

Mother was unhappy, Father was in prison, and she couldn't do anything to help. So she wrote a letter. And once more it was to the old gentleman.

Dear Friend,

Mother says we are not to ask for things for ourselves, but this isn't just for me.

You see what it says in this paper.

It isn't true. Father is not a spy.

Could you find out who did it, and then they would let Father out of prison.

Think if it was your Daddy, what would you feel? Please help me.

Love from your good friend,

Bobbie

Soon after she sent the letter, Bobbie had her twelfth birthday. Mother gave her a bracelet she no longer wore, Peter and Phyllis made a cake, and Mr. Perks brought a bunch of flowers from his garden.

It was very different from her last birthday when she'd had a huge party and lots of presents. This one was happy enough. But Bobbie missed Father so badly, her mind was filled with wanting him.

Then, one late summer's day, when the roses were out and the corn was ripening to gold, Bobbie found it impossible to concentrate on her lessons.

"Please, Mother," she begged. "Can I go outside?"

"Do you have a headache?" asked Mother.

Bobbie thought. "Not really," she replied.
"I just feel in a daze. I'd be more alive in
the fresh air, I think."

Mother let her go and Bobbie found herself
walking down to the station. She felt as if she
were in a dream.

At the station, everyone smiled at her and Mr. Perks shook her hand up and down.

"I saw it in the papers," he grinned. "I'm so pleased. And here comes the 11:54 London train, right on time."

"Saw what in the papers?" Bobbie asked, puzzled, but Mr. Perks had turned away, blowing his whistle.

As the train drew into the station, Bobbie was astonished to see handkerchiefs fluttering from every window.

Only three people got out. An old woman with a basket of squawking hens, the grocer's wife with some brown-paper packages, and the third...

"Oh! My Daddy, my Daddy!" Bobbie's cry pierced the air.

People looked out of the windows to see a tall
thin man and a little girl rush up to each other
with open arms.

"I felt something strange was going to happen today," said Bobbie as they walked up the hill, "but I never guessed what."

"Didn't Mother get my letter?" Father asked.
"There weren't any letters this morning," Bobbie replied.

"Mother wrote to tell me you'd found out," he said. "You've been wonderful. The old gentleman has too. He helped them catch the real spy. Now, Bobbie, run ahead and tell Mother and Peter and Phyllis I'm home."

He paused in the garden, looking around at the rich summer countryside with the hungry eyes of someone who has seen too little of flowers and trees and the wide blue sky.

Mother, Bobbie, Peter and Phyllis stood in the doorway. Father went down the path to join them.

We won't follow him. In that happy moment, in that happy family, no one else is wanted just now.

# The Wizard of Oz

# L. Frank Baum (1856-1919)

L. Frank Baum grew up in a wealthy American family. He had several jobs before becoming a writer, including running a grocery store and breeding chickens. But he always loved telling stories – and people loved reading them. *The Wizard of Oz* was an instant hit when it was published, sparking off a whole series of books set in Oz, as well as a famous film.

# The Wizard of Oz

# Chapter 1
# The cyclone

Dorothy lived on a lonely farm in Kansas, with only her Uncle Henry, her Aunt Em and her little dog Toto for company. One day, as they played outside, the sky grew dark...

73

Then the wind whipped up, with a chilling moan.

"There's a cyclone coming," called her Uncle Henry. "Quick, into the cellar!"

In a panic, Toto ran to hide under her bed. Dorothy dashed after him, as the wind shrieked and the whole house shook.

74

With a mighty wrench, the cyclone whirled
the house into the sky. Dorothy shivered
with terror.

"What will happen to us, Toto?"
she whispered.

The house sailed through the sky for hours...
Suddenly, with a sickening jolt, they landed.

"Welcome to Oz," cried a man in a pointed
hat, "and thank you! You've just killed the
Wicked Witch of the East and
set us free."

"Who? What?" asked Dorothy, horrified. "I
haven't killed anyone."

"Well, your house did," a woman told her.
"Look!" Two scrawny legs stuck out from under
a wall.

As Dorothy looked, the legs vanished,
leaving only a pair of silvery shoes behind.
The woman handed them to Dorothy.

"These are yours now," she said.

Dorothy took the shoes in a daze.
"Do you know the way to Kansas?"
she asked. "I have to go home."
The strangers shook their heads.
"Maybe the Great Wizard can help,"
suggested the woman. "He lives
in Emerald City, at the end
of the yellow
brick road..."

# Chapter 2

## A scarecrow, a tinman and a lion

Emerald City

Dorothy packed some food and set out for the city at once. She walked briskly along the yellow road, her silver shoes tinkling on the bricks.

79

As she passed a field, a scarecrow winked at her. Dorothy jumped in surprise.

"How do you do?" he asked.

"He talks too!" thought Dorothy. "H-hello," she said, shyly. "How are you?"

"Not so good," the scarecrow said. "It's very boring stuck up here..."

"Where are you off to?" he asked, a moment later.

"To see the wizard," Dorothy replied. "I need help to get home."

"Wizard? What wizard?" said the scarecrow. "I don't know anything," he added sadly. "I have no brains."

"Oh dear," said Dorothy. "Well, why don't you come with me? Maybe the wizard could give you some brains."

So they went on together. The land grew wilder until, by evening, they were walking through a thick forest. That night, they sheltered in a log cabin.

Dorothy woke to hear strange groans. A man made of tin was standing, as still as a statue, by a pile of logs.

"Are you alright?" she asked.

"No!" the tinman grunted. "I can't move. I was caught in the rain and I've rusted."

Dorothy spotted an oil can and swiftly oiled the tinman's joints.

"Thank you," he sighed. "I might have stood there forever. What brings you here?"

"The scarecrow and I are going to see the Great Wizard," Dorothy told him. "I want to go home and the scarecrow wants a brain."

The tinman thought for a second. "Do you think the wizard could give me a heart?" he asked.

"I expect so," said Dorothy.

"Then I'll come too," he decided.

The new companions had just set off when a lion leaped onto the road. Opening his slobbery jaws, he gave a terrible roar.

As the lion towered over Toto, Dorothy smacked him on the nose.

"Stop it!" she cried. "You must be a coward to pick on a little dog."

The lion looked ashamed. "You're right," he mumbled. "I only roar to make people run away."

"You should ask the wizard for courage," said Dorothy and told him where they were going.

The lion nodded eagerly. "I'll come with you!" he growled.

# Chapter 3
# A dangerous journey

The companions strolled on to the edge of the forest, where a deep ditch barred their way.

"We're stuck," sighed the lion.

But the scarecrow had an idea. "If the tinman chops down this tree, we could use it to cross the ditch."

The tree made a perfect bridge. They were almost across when they heard fierce growls from behind.

"A tiger monster!" whimpered the lion. "We're all doomed..."

"Quick, tinman!" ordered the scarecrow. "Chop away the tree."

The tree bridge fell with a crash and the
monster plummeted into the ditch. Dorothy
and her friends hurried on. Soon, they arrived at
a broad river.

"We need a raft," declared the scarecrow, and
the tinman set to work once again.

The raft bobbed along happily until they reached the middle of the river. Here, the current was so strong, it swept them away.

"We'll never reach Emerald City," wailed the lion.

Diving into the water, he took hold of the raft and swam as hard as he could. Slowly, he pulled them ashore.

Safely over the river, they went on, through a field bursting with poppies. A spicy scent filled the air and Dorothy felt drowsy. She sank into the flowers and wouldn't wake.

"It's the poppies..." yawned the lion. "They've sent... her... to sleep."

Luckily, the tinman and the scarecrow – who weren't made of flesh – stayed wide awake.

"Run!" the scarecrow ordered the lion. "We'll bring Dorothy."

The lion bounded ahead, leaving the scarecrow and tinman to carry Dorothy and Toto from the field.

On and on the pair staggered. Almost at
the end of the poppies they passed the lion
– fast asleep.

Quickly, they laid Dorothy in the open air to
recover and went back. With much pushing and
pulling, grunting and groaning, they dragged
the lion to safety.

# Chapter 4
# Emerald City

The yellow brick road
stretched off into the distance, but on
the horizon, something sparkled. Soon,
a vast green city loomed ahead.
"We've made it!" said Dorothy.
"Look," added the lion, pointing to a gate
studded with emeralds.

94

Dorothy knocked on the gate and a man in a green uniform appeared.

"Yes?" he said.

"Please may we see the Great Wizard?" asked Dorothy.

"I can take you to his palace," said the man, "but you must wear glasses. Our city is dazzling." And he pulled out a pair of green glasses for each of them, including Toto.

Inside, the city was an incredible sight. The streets and houses were built of shining green marble and all the people wore green. The shops sold green popcorn, green hats and green shoes. Everything was green – even the sky.

The gatekeeper led them to a grand palace.

"We'd like to see the wizard," Dorothy told the soldier on guard.

"Enter one at a time," he barked. "You first."

Nervously, Dorothy went inside.

"I am the wizard," boomed a giant head. "Why do you seek me?"

Dorothy took a deep breath. "Can you send me home to Kansas?"

The head frowned. "Only if you do something for me first," it snapped. "Kill the Wicked Witch of the West. Now go!"

Then the scarecrow stepped in.

A lady with green wings was sitting on the throne. "I am the wizard," she said gently. "What do you seek?"

"I am only a scarecrow, stuffed with straw. I ask you for brains."

"Kill the Wicked Witch of the West and I'll give you what you want," she murmured.

The tinman saw a terrible beast with five eyes and five limbs.

"I am the wizard," roared the beast. "Why do you seek me?"

"I am made of tin and have no heart. Please give me a heart, so I can love and be happy," he begged. But he too was turned away, with the same command.

The lion went last. Now, above the throne, blazed a ball of fire.

"I am the wizard," hissed the ball. "Why do you seek me?"

"I am a c-c-coward," stammered the lion. "I want c-c-courage, so I may truly be King of the Beasts." But the Lion didn't fare any better than the others. He too was told to kill the Wicked Witch of the West.

Outside the palace, the friends were glum. "We can't defeat a witch," moaned the scarecrow.

"But we can try," said the lion. So they walked back to the gate.

"Good luck," said the gatekeeper, pointing out the path to the witch's castle. "You'll need it!"

# Chapter 5
# A wicked witch

The Wicked Witch of the West had only one eye, but it saw a long way. She spotted the friends as they left the city. "Strangers coming here?" she screeched. She blew a whistle and a pack of wolves ran up. "Tear the strangers to shreds," she said.

The wolves bared their teeth and dashed away.
Luckily, the tinman heard them coming.

As the first
wolf reached them,
he chopped off its head.
Again and again he swung his
hatchet, until all the wolves lay dead.

The witch scowled. She blew her whistle
twice and a flock of crows flew down. "Peck the
strangers to pieces," she snapped.

This time, the scarecrow saw them coming.
As the first crow flew at him, the scarecrow
grabbed him and wrung his neck. One by one,
he wrung the neck of every single crow.

Now the witch was furious. She blew three times on her whistle to fetch a swarm of bees. "Sting the strangers to death!" she screamed.

Quickly, the scarecrow scattered straw over Dorothy, Toto and the lion to hide them. The bees tried to attack the tinman instead, but they snapped their stingers on his hard, tin body and died.

The witch gnashed her teeth, but she had one last trick up her sleeve – a cap that gave its owner three wishes. The witch had one wish left.

As she put on the cap, a crowd of magic monkeys appeared in a rush of wings. "Kill the strangers!" she howled. "Except the lion. I want him as my slave."

The monkeys flew off and seized the friends. They pulled out the scarecrow's stuffing and dropped him in the trees. They threw the tinman onto a rocky plain, smashing him to pieces. And they tied up the lion to carry him to the castle.

But at Dorothy, they stopped. "We can't hurt her," they said. "Let's take her to the witch."

Dorothy didn't know it, but the silver shoes gave her great power. The witch gulped when she saw them... until she noticed how frightened Dorothy was.

"She doesn't know about the shoes!" the witch thought gleefully. "Do as I say, or I'll kill you," she screamed at Dorothy, and set her to work.

The lion was tied up outside. Dorothy couldn't see how they'd ever escape. Every way out was guarded by the witch's slaves.

110

But the witch had lost much of her power.
"My wolves, my crows, my bees... all dead," she
thought angrily. "Even
my cap has no more
wishes left. I need a
plan. I must steal
those silver
shoes."

Silently, the witch put an invisible iron bar on the ground. Dorothy tripped over it and one of her shoes flew off. The witch pounced on it.

"Give me back my shoe," said Dorothy crossly.

"Never," cackled the witch. "And I shall steal the other one too!"

112

Dorothy was so angry she threw a pail of water over the witch. At once, the witch began to shrink.

"Agh! I'm melting..." she wailed.

Soon, all that was left of the witch was a brown puddle and one silver shoe. Dorothy hastily put her shoe back on and raced out to the lion.

"The witch is dead!" she shouted.

# Chapter 6
## The wizard's trick

The witch's slaves danced with joy and helped
Dorothy and the lion look for their friends.
It didn't take long to find the battered
remains of the scarecrow and the tinman.

The tinman was soon put back together and after the scarecrow had been stuffed with fresh straw, he felt as good as new.

"Now," said Dorothy, "let's go and claim our rewards!" So they packed her basket with food from the witch's kitchen, covered it with a cloth cap and set off.

After several hours, they stopped for lunch.
"I can't wait to see the wizard," said Dorothy,
as she unpacked the basket. "I wish we were
in Emerald City now." Suddenly, there was a
fluttering of wings and, to everyone's surprise,
the magic monkeys appeared.

All at once, the friends were flying through the air. "The cloth cap must be a wishing cap," Dorothy gasped.

Before long, they could see the shining roofs of Emerald City. The monkeys set them down and flew away.

The wizard kept them waiting for ages. Finally, a soldier with a green beard ushered them in.

This time, the room was empty, but a voice echoed, "I am the wizard. Why do you seek me?"

"To claim our rewards," said the friends. "The Wicked Witch is dead."

"But..." began the voice.

"We want our rewards!" roared the lion. Toto jumped in fright and knocked over a screen in the corner...

118

...to reveal a little old man, with fuzzy hair and glasses.

"Who are you?" demanded the tinman, waving his hatchet.

"I'm the wizard," croaked the man. "But you can call me Oz."

"What about the head – the lady – the beast – the ball of fire?" cried the friends.

"Um, they were tricks," Oz said, sheepishly. "I'm not a real wizard. I'm not even from here. I was in a hot-air balloon that blew off-course. Since I appeared from the sky, the people thought I was a wizard."

"They asked me to rule them and I built Emerald City. Isn't it green?" Oz asked proudly. "Of course, you have to wear green-tinted glasses for the full effect," he admitted.

"The witches were my only fear. I was so glad when your house killed the first one. I would have said anything to get rid of the other."

"But what about our rewards?" asked the friends together.

"You don't need them," Oz replied. "Scarecrow, you're full of ideas. Lion, you're brave, you just lack confidence. And Tinman, hearts make most people unhappy."

"But you promised!" they said.

Oz sighed. "I'll do my best."

"And can you send me home?" Dorothy asked.

"I'll try," Oz replied.

# Chapter 7
# Oz's rewards

Oz summoned everyone the very next day. "Scarecrow first," he said.

He took the scarecrow's head and tipped in a handful of pins. "This will make you as sharp as a pin!"

And the scarecrow felt very wise.

Next came the tinman. "Here's your heart," said Oz, giving him a heart-shaped cushion. "It's a very kind one." The tinman beamed.

Then Oz produced a green bottle. "This is courage," he told the lion.

The lion gulped it down. "Now I feel brave!" he roared.

Finally, Oz led
Dorothy to a basket.
"I mended my balloon,"
he said.
"We'll
fly home!"

He lit a fire and hot air swelled the balloon.
The basket began to lift.

"Hurry!" Oz cried to Dorothy – but she was
looking for Toto. She swept him up and ran to
the basket.

Just as she reached it, a rope snapped and the
balloon took off.

"Come back!" she called. It was too late.
"Now I'll never get home," she wept. Her
friends hated to see her so unhappy. The
scarecrow racked his new brains.

"I know," he said. "Wish for the magic monkeys to take you!"

But they couldn't help. "We can't leave this land," they explained.

Then a soldier spoke up. "Why not ask the Good Witch Glinda?"

So Dorothy and her friends set off once more.

# Chapter 8
# Home again

Glinda lived far in the south. It would have been a difficult journey without the cap's third wish.

"Please take us to Glinda," said Dorothy and the monkeys carried them to a beautiful castle.

"What can I do for you?" Glinda asked her visitors kindly.

Dorothy told her the whole story. "And now I just want to go home," she finished.

"Bless you," said Glinda, smiling. "I'm sure I can get you all home. But I'll need the wishing cap."

She turned to the others. "What will you do when Dorothy leaves?"

"I'll live in Emerald City," the scarecrow told her.

"I'll go back to my cabin," said the tinman.

"And I'll go home to the forest," added the lion.

"I'll ask the monkeys to take you all where you wish," said Glinda. "Then I'll set them free."

"You're very kind," said Dorothy, "but please, how can I get home?"

"Your silver shoes will take you," replied Glinda. "Just knock the heels together three times and say where you want to go."

With glistening eyes, Dorothy said goodbye to her friends. Then she hugged Toto tightly and clicked her heels together.

"Take me home!" she cried.

At once, she was whirling through the air... and rolling on the soft grass of a familiar field.

Aunt Em dropped her
watering can and rushed over.
"My darling child!" she said,
covering Dorothy with kisses.
"Wherever did you come
from?"

"From Oz," said
Dorothy. "And oh, Aunt
Em, I'm so glad to be
home!"

# The Secret Garden

# Frances Hodgson Burnett (1849-1924)

Born in England in 1849, Frances moved to America
with her family when she was 16. A year later, Frances
sold her first story. She went on to become one of the
most famous children's writers of all time.
Her other books include *A Little Princess*
and *Little Lord Fauntleroy*.

# Chapter 1
# Contrary Mary

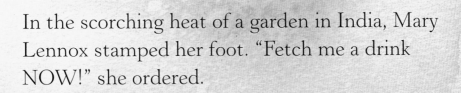

In the scorching heat of a garden in India, Mary
Lennox stamped her foot. "Fetch me a drink
NOW!" she ordered.

137

Instantly, servants rushed to obey.
Meanwhile, Mary began to make a pretend
garden, sticking flowers into the hot dry earth.
"It looks all wrong," she muttered.

Glancing up, Mary saw a beautiful woman
strolling past, surrounded by an admiring group
of army officers.

138

"Mother!" cried Mary. She rushed forward, but Mrs. Lennox brushed her daughter away, as she always did.

It was Mary's last glimpse of her mother. Over the next few days a terrible fever, cholera, swept through her parents' house.

Her mother and father died, along with many of their servants.

Mary, shut away in the nursery, never caught the cholera. But she was left all alone in the world.

After that, Mary was passed around like a package between her parents' friends, until a letter came from her uncle, Mr. Craven.

Misselthwaite Manor,
Yorkshire, England

Dear Mary,

I have made arrangements for you to come to England and live at Misselthwaite Manor. My housekeeper, Mrs. Medlock, will meet you in London and escort you here.

I'm afraid I won't see you for some time as I have to travel to Europe on business.

Yours sincerely,

Archibald Craven

"No one cares what I want," Mary thought, but she had nowhere else to go.

# Chapter 2
## The strange house

Several weeks later, Mary was sitting in a
freezing cold carriage, opposite the
stern-looking Mrs. Medlock.

"What's that whooshing noise?" Mary asked, as they drove across a bleak landscape.

"It's the wind howling across the moor," Mrs. Medlock replied.

"What's a moor?" asked Mary.

"Miles of empty land – and the manor is right in the middle of it."

"I hate it already," thought Mary.

"How many servants will I have?" she asked.

Mrs. Medlock looked shocked. "I don't know how it was in India," she said, "but here you'll take care of yourself."

They arrived late at night. Mrs. Medlock marched Mary across a huge hall, up steep stairs and along twisting corridors.

"Your bedroom," she announced, at last, flinging open a door. "You must stay here, unless you're going outside. On no account must you go poking around the house."

As soon as Mary stepped into the room, Mrs. Medlock left, shutting the door behind her before hurrying off.

Mary looked around. It was not a child's
room. Tapestries hung on the walls and in the
middle stood a vast four-poster bed.

Outside the wind howled like a lonely person, as lonely as Mary. Then another noise pierced the wind – a far-off sobbing sound.

"That's not the wind," Mary thought. "It's a child crying. Who is it?"

She was itching with curiosity, but she didn't dare disobey Mrs. Medlock. Finally, worn out from her journey, she fell asleep.

# Chapter 3
## A robin and a key

The next morning, Mrs. Medlock bustled into Mary's room with her breakfast.

"Ugh!" exclaimed Mary, looking at the porridge. "What's that? It looks disgusting. I won't eat it."

Mrs. Medlock sighed at the pale, skinny child, swamped by the big bed. "Just drink your milk then," she said, "and you can go out."

"Don't want to," retorted Mary.

"Well, if you don't, you'll be stuck in here and there's nothing to do inside," snapped Mrs. Medlock.

Mary took a while to get dressed – she'd always had servants to dress her before – but finally she was ready.

Mrs. Medlock showed her the way to the gardens and she wandered out, past wide lawns, wintry flower beds and trees clipped into strange shapes.

The only person she could see was an old man digging.

"Who are you?" demanded Mary.

"Ben Weatherstaff," he growled.

"What's in there?" Mary asked, pointing to a crumbling, ivy-covered wall behind them.

"Ah," said Ben. "That's the secret garden. Mr. Craven shut it up."

"Why?" asked Mary.

Ben looked sad. "It was Mrs. Craven's special garden and she loved it. But she died and the master was so unhappy, he buried the key and went away."

As he spoke, a robin flew up to Ben. His wrinkled face creased into a smile.

"There's no door," Ben went on, "but that doesn't stop this one."

The robin cocked its head to the side and looked at Mary. Enchanted, she whispered, "Will you be friends with me?"

"So..." Ben murmured. "You can be friendly, after all. You sound just like Dickon talking to his animals."

"Who's Dickon?" asked Mary.

"He's the brother of a maid here," said Ben. "Dickon can grow flowers out of stones and charm the birds. Even the deer love young Dickon."

"I wish I could meet him!"

But Ben was growing impatient. "Run along now," he said. "I've got work to do."

The robin flew off. Mary followed him. "Please, robin, show me the way to the garden," she begged.

The robin chirruped and hopped up and down on the ground.

"He's telling me something," thought Mary. She scrabbled in the soil and saw, half-hidden, a rusty ring. Picking it up, she saw it wasn't a ring at all. It was a key. The key to the secret garden.

# Chapter 4
# Dickon

Every morning, Mary jumped out of bed, ready to search for a way into the garden.

"I have the key," she told herself. "I just need to find the door."

157

Mrs. Medlock noticed a change in her. "She looks downright pretty now, with her rosy cheeks," she thought. "She was so plain and scrawny at first."

One day, as the winter trees were beginning to blossom and the wind came in sweet-scented gusts from the moor, the robin fluttered down and hopped along beside Mary.

Mary never knew if what happened next was magic. A gust of wind lifted up a patch of ivy to reveal an old wooden door.
Mary put her key in the lock, turned it with both hands and pushed.
Slowly, the door creaked open...

She was inside the secret garden!

It was a mysterious place – a hazy, frosty tangle of rose branches that trailed the walls and spread along the ground.

Hundreds of green spiky shoots thrust up through withered grass.

"It isn't completely dead," she whispered. "I am glad."

The shoots looked so crowded that she began to clear spaces around them. The robin chirped, as though pleased someone was gardening here at last.

Mary worked for hours. "It must be lunchtime," she thought, hungrily. "I'd better go in, before Mrs. Medlock starts looking for me."

Racing back after lunch, she noticed Ben talking to a curly-haired boy, with a fawn by his side. As the boy walked away, he played a tune on a rough wooden pipe.

Shyly, Mary went up to him. "Are you Dickon?"

"I am," he grinned. "And you're Mary. Ben told me about you."

He looked so friendly and kind, Mary felt she
could trust him. "Can you keep a secret?"

Dickon chuckled. "I keep secrets all the time.
If I told where wild animals live and birds make
their nests, they wouldn't be safe."

"I've found the secret garden," she said quickly.

"I think it's mostly dead. I'm the only person who wants it to live. Come and see."

She led him through the ivy curtain and Dickon looked around, amazed. "I never thought I'd see this place," he murmured. "It's like being in a dream."

He scraped a rose branch with his pocket knife. "There's green underneath," he said. "These roses are alive. Some dead wood needs cutting, that's all."

Mary danced around the garden in delight.

"It'll be a fountain of roses, come summer," said Dickon. "We'll add more plants too – snapdragons, larkspur, love-in-a-mist. We'll have the prettiest garden in England."

"Will you really help?" asked Mary. She could hardly believe it.

"Of course," he replied. "It's fun, shut in here, waking up a garden."

# Chapter 5
# A cry in the night

Every day they worked in the garden.

"I don't want it too tidy," Mary decided. "It wouldn't feel like a secret garden then."

"It's secret, sure enough," said Dickon. "Look
– the robin's building a nest. He wouldn't do
that, unless he felt safe."

"I feel safe and happy here, too," Mary
confided. "But I used to be angry all the time.
Nobody liked me."

Dickon's fawn nuzzled Mary's hand and he laughed. "There's someone who likes you," he said. "So does the robin and so do I."

That night, lying in bed, Mary heard the wind rage.

"I don't hate it now," she realized.

She thought of the wild animals on the moor, snuggled in their holes, protected from its blasts.

Suddenly, she was alert, listening.

"There's that noise again," she thought. "Crying. It's definitely not the wind. Where's it coming from?"

Gripping her bedside candle, she followed
the sound down shadowy passages, until she
reached a door with a glimmer of light beneath.

Quietly, she opened the door. A fire burning in the grate threw a dim light onto a huge carved bed. In the bed was a boy, sobbing. Dark eyes stared from an ivory-white face.

"Are you a ghost?" he whimpered.

"No," said Mary. "Are you?"

"I'm Colin Craven," said the boy.

Mary gasped. "Mr. Craven's my uncle. I'm Mary Lennox."

"Well, Mr. Craven's my father," said Colin.

Mary looked at him in astonishment. "Why didn't Mrs. Medlock tell me about you?"

"I don't let people talk about me," Colin said, "because I'm going to die."

Mary was horrified. "What's wrong with you?"
Colin sighed. "I'm weak."
"You won't die from that," Mary scoffed.

"And my father doesn't even care," Colin went
on, as if he hadn't heard. "He hates me because
my mother died when I was born. He can't bear
to look at me."

"Just like the secret garden," Mary said.

"What garden?"

"Your mother's garden," Mary explained.
"Your father shut it up after she died."

"I'll have it unlocked,"
Colin announced grandly.
"No!" cried Mary.
"Why not?"

"Then *everyone* would go in it. It wouldn't be a secret any more!"

"Never mind," said Colin, fretfully. "I'll never see it anyway."

"Yes you will!" argued Mary. "You go outside, don't you?"

"Never," said Colin. "I can't cope with cold air. Don't forget I'm dying."

Mary felt he was rather proud of this and she didn't like it. "Don't talk about death all the time," she said. "Think of other things."

Her voice dropped to a whisper. "Think of the sun and rain and buds bursting into flower. Think of new green leaves. Think of the secret garden, coming alive…"

Gradually, Colin's eyes closed, and Mary crept away.

# Chapter 6
# The magic of the garden

The next morning Mary had to see if she'd
dreamed it all. She burst into Colin's room and
pulled back the curtains, flooding the room
with sunlight.

Colin sat up in bed and smiled. "I've just realized," he said. "We're cousins!"

They were talking so loudly they didn't hear Mrs. Medlock come in.

"I told you not to go poking around," she shouted at Mary. "Go back to your room at once."

"No," Colin ordered. "I like her. I want her to stay with me."

"She'll tire you out," said Mrs. Medlock. "Come along, Mary."

"DO WHAT I SAY!" screamed Colin. "Leave Mary and get out."

"Yes, dear," said Mrs. Medlock, trying to sound soothing. She'd promised Mr. Craven she would never upset Colin. Hurriedly, she withdrew.

"You're horribly bossy," said Mary. "I used to be like that, when I lived in India. But I'm trying to change now."

"Why shouldn't I give orders?" snapped Colin. "I'm master of this house when Father's away." Mary got up to leave.

"Don't go!" pleaded Colin, all trace of bossiness gone from his voice.

"I don't want to be alone."

"I'll be back later," Mary promised. "I have a friend I want you to meet."

A few hours later, Mary and Dickon crept into
Colin's room.

"You've been ages," complained Colin, scowling at them.

"Say hello to Dickon," said Mary. "I want you to come out with us. I want to show you a secret."

"The garden?" guessed Colin.

Mary nodded.

"I'll come," he decided and rang a bell to summon Mrs. Medlock.

"I'm going outside," he stated. "Bring my wheelchair. And tell everyone to keep away."

"Are you sure, dear?" she asked, anxiously. "You'll catch cold."

"Just do as I say," Colin ordered.

Dickon pushed Colin along the paths until Mary stopped and, flinging back the ivy, opened the garden door.

Sunshine lit up sprays of flowers and the air was alive with birdsong.

Colin stared. "I can *feel* things growing," he gasped.

"It's spring," said Dickon. "Makes you feel good. We'll soon have you working in the garden."

"But I can't even stand," Colin faltered, looking at his thin legs.

"Only because you haven't tried," said Mary.

Dickon helped Colin to his feet.

"Try now, Colin. You can walk, you really can," urged Mary.

Unsteadily and clinging to Dickon, Colin forced his weak limbs to move. The others saw his pale face grow rosy in the sunlight.

"Mary! Dickon!" he cried. "I'm going to get well. I can feel it."

# Chapter 7
# Mr. Craven comes home

Every day they played and worked in the garden
and, every day, Colin grew stronger.

By the time spring turned into summer, he was completely well. But the three of them pretended he was still ill.

"No one must know," Colin insisted. "I want to surprise my father. If only he'd come home..."

Colin began to wish, "Come home, come home."

One night, Colin's father, far away in Italy, had a strange dream. He heard his dead wife calling his name.

"Where are you?" he pleaded.

"In the garden," came the reply, like the sound from a golden flute.

Mr. Craven woke, determined to return to his manor at once.

"Where's Colin?" he demanded, the minute he arrived home.

Mrs. Medlock gasped, shocked at his sudden appearance.

"He plays in the garden, sir, with Mary and Dickon," she said in a shaky voice. "No one is allowed near them."

"In the garden?" thought Mr. Craven.
"My dream..."

As he hurried down the path, he heard
children laughing in his wife's old garden.

"The door's locked and the key's buried," he told himself. "I must still be dreaming."

Suddenly, the door burst open and Colin and Mary dashed out.

"Father! You're here!" cried Colin.

196

Mr. Craven hugged his son tight. "Is it really you? You're well! However did it happen?"

"It was the garden," said Colin. "And Mary."

"I thought the garden would be dead," murmured his father.

"It came alive," said Mary.

Mr. Craven smiled. "And so has Colin," he said. "Thank you, Mary."

# Black Beauty

# Anna Sewell (1820-1878)

Anna Sewell adored horses. She suffered from a bone disease and, after spraining her ankle as a young girl, she became increasingly lame. For the last six years of her life, she couldn't move from her house. She longed to make people more caring about horses, so she wrote *Black Beauty* (her only book), lying on her sofa. Anna died just after it was published, never knowing its success.

# Chapter 1
## In the beginning

When I was very young my life was gloriously
happy. I galloped with other colts by day and
slept by my mother's side at night.

But when I was four years old, a man named Squire Gordon came to talk to my master, the horse breeder.

He stroked my black coat and the white star on my forehead. "Beautiful!" he exclaimed. "Break him in and I'll buy him!"

Then he touched the white patch on my back. "It's like a beauty spot," he said. "I'll call him Black Beauty."

I shook with fear. I was going to be sold! Would I have to leave my mother? And what was *breaking in*?

"You must learn to wear a saddle and bridle," my mother explained. Then the groom thrust a cold steel bar into my mouth and held it there, with straps over my head and under my throat. There was no escape.

At first the bar frightened me, but with kind words and treats of oats I learned to get used to it.

Just before I was taken to Squire Gordon, my mother spoke to me for the last time. "Now, Black Beauty," she whispered, "be brave. All young horses must leave their mothers to make their way in the world."

"Just remember – never bite or rear or kick. And whatever happens, always do your best."

When Squire Gordon's groom arrived, he
jumped on my back and we rode away.
I cantered through twisting villages
until we reached a long drive.
Apple orchards stretched out
on either side.

The groom led me into a large, airy stable
with plenty of corn and hay. A friendly whinny
from the next stall made me look up.

A fat little pony with a thick mane and tail was poking his head over the rail. "I'm Merrylegs," he said. "Welcome to Birtwick Park."

"That was John who rode you here," Merrylegs went on. "He's the best groom around – and Squire Gordon is the best owner a horse could have. You'll be happy here."

A tall chestnut mare glared at Merrylegs. "Trouble is, no one knows how long a good home will last," she snapped. "I've had more homes than you've had hot oats."

"Meet Ginger," said Merrylegs. "She bites. That's why she keeps getting sold, even though she's so handsome."

Angrily, Ginger tore at wisps of hay in her manger. "You don't know anything," she muttered. "If you'd been through what I have, you'd bite too."

"Poor Ginger!" I thought. "What could have made her so unhappy?"

# Chapter 2
## Ginger's story

Over the next few days, John took me out.
At first we went slowly... then we trotted and
cantered, and ended up in a wonderful
speedy gallop.

"Well, John, how is my new horse?" asked Squire Gordon.

"First rate, Sir," replied John, grooming me carefully. "Black Beauty's as swift as a deer, as gentle as a dove and as safe as houses."

"A lady's horse, perhaps?" asked the Squire's wife, feeding me pieces of apple.

"Oh yes, Mrs. Gordon. He'll be a good carriage horse too. We could try him out with Ginger," John suggested.

So I was paired up with Ginger to pull the carriage. During our journeys, she told me the story of her life.

"If I'd had your upbringing, I might be good tempered like you," she began. "My first memory is of a stone being thrown at me."

"Poor you!" I said, but Ginger hadn't finished.
"When my first owner broke me in, he shoved
a painful bit in my mouth," she went on.

"I reared up in pain and he fought me with his
whip until blood poured from my flanks...

...and then he cut off my tail."

"Why?" I cried. I'd noticed Ginger had no tail, but thought she must have lost it in an accident.

"Fashion," Ginger replied bitterly. "Some people think horses look better with a stump. Now I have nothing to whisk flies away with."

She sighed. "It's agony when they crawl on me and sting."

"Horrible!" I snorted.

"That's not all. My first owner sold me to a rich London gentleman who put me in a bearing rein."

"A what?" I asked.

"It's a tight rein that pulls your neck all the way back. Imagine your tongue pinched, your jaw jerked upright and your neck on fire with pain.

Everyone thought I looked wonderful, but oh, how it hurt! Kindness wins us, not painful whips," said Ginger.

"But we're lucky here," she said, at last. "Squire Gordon hates bearing reins, and John is teaching young Joe, our new groom, to be just as good as he is.

And I'm *trying* to behave now, because everyone's so kind."

# Chapter 3
# Horses know best

Soon after this, Mrs. Gordon fell ill. We didn't see her for weeks. Then one stormy night John rushed to the stables.

"Best foot forward, Beauty," he cried. "We must ride as hard as we can to fetch the doctor. Mrs. Gordon is at death's door."

We galloped into lashing rain, while thunder and lightning raged around us.

Leaves and twigs danced in the air, torn from their branches by a savage wind.

As we got to the main road, a terrible splitting sound crashed through the darkness. A huge tree had fallen in our path.

Gathering all my strength, I jumped – and sailed over it.

At last we reached the bridge. I could hear the river roaring. But the moment I stepped onto the bridge, I stopped.

"Come on, Beauty," John urged.

I couldn't move. I could tell something was wrong. John gave me a light touch of the whip, but I stayed like a statue.

Just then, the moon lit up the bridge. We saw the far end had collapsed into matchsticks, tossing in the raging water.

"Well done, Beauty!" John cried. "We would have been killed. But I'm afraid it's ten miles to the next bridge. We'll have to hurry."

"Gallop and get there…" I murmured to myself. "Gallop and get there…" The faster I said it, the faster I went.

I raced home with both John and the doctor on my back. I'd never been so tired in my life.

"You're steaming like a kettle," said young Joe. "You're too hot for your blanket. Here, have some ice-cold water."

All through the night I shivered and sweated and longed for John to come. When he arrived, he was horrified. "Joe! You've nearly killed Beauty!" he shouted. "He's caught a bad chill.

You should have put on his blanket – and that icy drink did him no good at all."

"I didn't know," Joe muttered sulkily.

"Didn't know?" yelled John. "You should make it your business to know. If you don't know, ask!"

"I'm sorry," wept Joe. "I didn't mean to hurt him. Will he die?"

"Let's hope not," replied John.

With careful nursing, I recovered, but Joe never forgot the lesson he had learned.

# Chapter 4
# A terrible time

Mrs. Gordon got better too, but the doctor said she must live in the sun to be really well.

Everything was to be sold – Birtwick Park, Merrylegs, Ginger and me. Merrylegs went to the priest, who'd promised to keep him for good.

We said goodbye under the apple trees, where we'd talked and played so happily. I never saw Merrylegs again.

Ginger and I were sold to Lord and Lady
Richmore. John had tears in his eyes when he
handed us over to Reuben, our new groom.

The next day, Lord and Lady
Richmore came to inspect us.

"They look very nice, Reuben," announced
Lady Richmore. "They can pull my carriage.
But you must put their heads up. High."

"Squire Gordon never used a bearing rein," Lord Richmore reminded her.

"Well, I won't have horrible, common-looking horses," snapped Lady Richmore.

Reuben pulled my head back and fixed the rein tight. I felt red-hot pain. Ginger tried to jerk her head away, but Reuben forced her rein like mine.

Instantly, I saw why Ginger hated it. I couldn't put my head down to take the strain of pulling the carriage. As the strength drained out of us, Reuben whipped us on.

At last, we came to a
grand courtyard crammed
with horses and carriages.
Ginger couldn't take it
any more.

With a wild neigh she reared up, scaring all
the horses who crashed into each other, kicking
madly. Our carriage toppled over and broke
to pieces.

Lady Richmore tumbled out, unharmed but furious.

Ginger was taken away forever. I longed to know what happened to her, but no one mentioned her name again.

I didn't trust Reuben. He oozed politeness to the Richmores, but secretly he drank too much.

One evening, he took me out for a ride on a road made of fresh-laid sharp stones. My shoe was loose, but Reuben was too drunk to notice.

He never heard the clatter of my shoe falling off. I don't think he even noticed me limping. My hoof split and – I couldn't help it! I fell onto my knees. Reuben shot to the ground, hit his head on the cobbles and lay there, not moving.

I stayed with Reuben all through the night. When morning dawned, a group of early walkers came by. They were shocked at the sight of us.

"That's Reuben," they shouted. "Dead, poor bloke. Thrown by that horse! Vicious brute! That'll be the end of him."

No one knew what really happened. And what would they do to me now?

# Chapter 5
## Life is a puzzle

"I'm going to sell that bad-tempered Black Beauty to any fool who wants him," Lord Richmore announced.

I was sorry for Reuben, but I couldn't
help being thrilled to be leaving Lord and
Lady Richmore.

I was put into a horse sale. Buyers prodded me and stared at me, but no one wanted me.

"Isn't he ugly with those nasty knees?" I heard someone say.

Finally a kind-looking man paid a small sum of money for me and took me away.

The man's name was Jerry Barker and he lived in London with his wife and children – Harry and the twins, Polly and Molly.

"I want you to be my cab horse," Jerry told me. "I'll call you Jack."

It was strange to have a new name. My job was to be harnessed to Jerry's carriage, which he called his cab, and pick up passengers when they hailed us in the street.

We worked hard, out all day in all weather – rain, sleet, snow and ice – with hardly any rest.

I didn't mind anything because Jerry was such a kind, honest man. I wanted to do my best for him.

He made sure I was always comfortable and had plenty of food. He never whipped me to go faster, even if customers in a hurry bribed him with extra cash.

"You'll never be rich!" the other cab drivers jeered.

"I have enough, thanks," Jerry replied. "It's not fair on Jack to make him hurry all the time."

Other cab horses weren't so lucky. I often saw them exhausted and miserable, made old before their time with too much work.

Once I saw an old, worn-out chestnut, with a thin neck and bones that stuck out through a badly-kept coat. Its eyes had a dull, hopeless look.

I was wondering why the horse looked faintly familiar when I heard a whisper.

"Black Beauty, is that you?"

It was Ginger! Her beautiful looks had completely vanished.

She told me she belonged to a cruel driver who whipped her, starved her and overworked her.

"You used to stand up for yourself if people were mean to you," I said.

"Yes, I did once, but now I'm too tired," she replied. "I just wish I could die."

"No, Ginger!" I cried. "Keep going! Better times will come."

"I hope they do for you, Black Beauty," she whispered. "Goodbye and good luck."

Soon after that meeting I saw a cart carrying a dead chestnut horse. It was a dreadful sight.

I think it was Ginger. I almost hope it was, for that meant her suffering was over.

# Chapter 6
# An unexpected ending

One day, a customer of Jerry's made him an offer he couldn't refuse. She asked him to be her groom at her house in the country.

"There's a little cottage for you and your family," she said. "I wish I could take Jack too, but I already have a horse."

"Sorry, old Jack," Jerry comforted me. "I hope someone kind will buy you."

But my new master was a cruel man. I
had to pull his carts loaded with sacks of corn,
and if I was too slow, he whipped me hard. He
hardly fed me either, which made me weak.

In the end I simply collapsed in the street.
"Stupid horse!" my master grunted. "Is he
dead? What a waste of money."

I couldn't move. As I lay there barely breathing, someone came up and poured water down my throat. A gentle voice said, "He's not dead, only exhausted."

The gentle voice belonged to a horse doctor. I couldn't believe my luck! The doctor helped me to my feet, and led me to his stables, where he gave me a warm mash.

"I think you were a good horse once," said the doctor, "though you're a poor, broken-down old thing now. I'm going to feed you up and find you a nice home."

Rest, good food and gentle exercise worked
on me like magic. But when the doctor said I
was ready to leave him, I trembled all over. I
dreaded to think what my next home would
be like.

The doctor took me to a pretty house in a small village. It had a pasture and a comfortable stable, and belonged to two grown-up sisters, Claire and Elspeth Lyefield.

"I'm sure we'll like you," they said, patting me. "You have such a gentle face." I nuzzled them, but I wasn't sure I could trust them.

Their groom led me to the stable and began
to clean me. "That white star is just like Black
Beauty's," he said, "and the glossy black coat.
He's about the same height too. I wonder where
Black Beauty is now?"

Soon he came to the tiny knot of white hair on my back. "That's what Squire Gordon called Beauty's patch. It is Black Beauty! It really is! Do you remember me? Young Joe who nearly killed you?"

I was so glad to see him! I've never seen a man so happy, either.

I've been here now for a year. Joe is always gentle, Claire and Elspeth are kind, and my work is easy. All my strength has come back and I've never been happier.

The sisters have promised never to sell me. Finally I've found my home, for ever and ever.

# Little Women

# Louisa May Alcott (1832-1888)

Louisa was born in Pennsylvania, USA
on November 29, 1832. Like her character, Jo March,
young Louisa was a tomboy. "No boy could be my friend
till I had beaten him in a race," she claimed.
Louisa loved to write. In all, she published over 30 books
and short stories, but is best remembered for *Little Women*.
As well as writing, Louisa spent time in Europe, served
as a nurse in the American Civil War and campaigned
for women's rights. She never married and died
in 1888, aged 55.

# Chapter 1
# A Christmas letter

"Christmas won't be Christmas without any presents," grumbled Jo March, lying on the rug.

"I hate being poor," sighed her sister, Meg, looking at her old dress.

"So do I," sniffed Amy, the youngest, who was gazing at passers-by. "And I don't think it's fair for some girls to have lots of pretty things and other girls nothing at all."

"At least we have Father and Mother and each other," said Beth.

"We don't have Father," Jo observed, moving to the sofa. "Not for a long time..."

"Perhaps never," each sister added silently to herself, thinking of their father far away at the war.

"Mother said we really ought not to have presents this Christmas anyway," announced Meg. "She thinks it's wrong to spend money for fun when our men are suffering in the army."

At sixteen, and the eldest, Meg did her best to sound grown-up, but she didn't always succeed.

"I'm sure Mother wouldn't want us to give up everything!" cried Jo. "And we each have a dollar. We could spend that on ourselves. I'm going to buy a book."

"I'll buy drawing paper," decided Amy.

Beth began playing the old piano, skipping over the parts where the notes were missing. "A new piano's too expensive," she said quietly, "but I'd love more music."

"We deserve some fun," Jo added. "I suffer enough every day looking after Great Aunt March with her fussy old woman ways."

"It can't be as bad as my job, teaching those horrible children," Meg complained. "I hate having to work."

"My life's worse," Amy butted in. "All the girls at school laugh at me because of my patched clothes."

Beth put her mother's old slippers to warm by the fire. They were full of holes. "Let's not get anything for ourselves," she said. "Let's buy presents for Mother instead. She works so hard."

Jo beamed. "That's a much better idea. We'll go shopping tomorrow." And, seizing Beth, she danced around the room.

Meg and Amy clapped and cheered them on. As the pair collapsed in an exhausted heap, they heard the front door open. Mother was home.

"I'm glad to find you so merry," she smiled, "I'm sorry I'm late. There was so much to do, sending food and clothes to our soldiers. But I have a treat – a letter from Father!"

Excitedly, they drew close. Their mother sat in
the big chair by the fire, and the girls clustered
around her. Jo perched by her feet, resting her
chin in her hand.

Father's letter was cheerful and full of hope.

It seems a long time to wait before I see you again. Give the girls my love. I know they will be loving children, that they will work hard and conquer their faults, so that when I return I will be fonder and prouder than ever of my little women.

# Chapter 2
## The Laurence boy

After Christmas, everyone felt miserable. "Nothing nice ever happens to us," moaned Amy.

"That's not true," said Jo, coming into the room and tripping over Beth's cat. In her fall, she knocked ink onto Meg's hat, leaving a dark, spreading stain.

"Oh, it's ruined!" snapped Meg. "And I can't afford another. You are so clumsy, Jo! Beth, can't you keep that cat of yours under control?"

272

Jo shrugged her shoulders. "Was there ever such a cross family? But just wait. One day I'll be writing books and plays and be so rich that I can buy stacks of hats. Beth can have all the cats in the world and a new piano."

"Meg! Jo!" their mother called, coming in from the hall. "This will cheer you up – a party invitation has arrived for a New Year's Eve dance tomorrow."

"If only I had a silk dress to wear," sighed Meg, later. "Mother says I have to wait until I'm eighteen, and that's two years away."

"Your dress is fine," said Jo. "My party dress is scorched where I stood too near the fire and my gloves have lemonade all over them."

"You can't wear them then," said Meg firmly. "We'll each wear one of my good gloves and hold one of yours. And you must make sure you keep your back out of sight or sit."

"I think I'm going to hate this party," Jo muttered.

Amy stuck out her bottom lip. "At least you're going. I wish I could."

"I'm glad I'm not," murmured Beth. "But I'm sure it'll be better than you think," she whispered to Jo.

The next evening, Jo helped Meg get ready, holding red-hot curling tongs to her hair. But soon she was thinking about her latest idea for a story... and a minute later she smelled burning.

To Meg's horror, a row of scorched curls fell onto her lap.

"Oh I can't do anything right!" said Jo, flinging down the tongs in disgust and rushing out of the room. Amy ran to console Meg.

"There," she said, fixing a velvet bow to Meg's hair. "Now it won't show."

As soon as they arrived at the party, Meg began dancing with her friends. Jo, who was terrified of showing Meg up, shot behind a curtain. To her surprise, she found a boy already there.

"You're Mr. Laurence's grandson," she blurted
out. "I've seen you before. You live next door
to us."

The boy nodded. "Hello," he said. "I'm Laurie.
I'm hiding because I hardly know anyone here."

"You know me now," said Jo, with a grin. "I'm
hiding because of my dress," she confessed,
showing him the burn.

Laurie laughed.

"Let's dance a polka down the passage where
no one will see us," he suggested.

After their dance, Laurie went to get ice creams, which they devoured behind the curtain. By the time the party ended they were firm friends.

They were laughing in a corner when Meg limped over to them. "These wretched shoes!" she groaned. "I think I've sprained my ankle."

"Would you like a lift in my carriage?" Laurie offered.

"If it won't be too much trouble," said Meg. "Yes please!"

Mrs. March was still up when they arrived home, waiting to hear about the party. When she saw Meg, she fussed around her like a mother hen.

"We came back with Mr. Laurence's grandson," Jo said, as Mrs. March bandaged Meg's ankle.

"He's an orphan," their mother told them. "He's only just moved in with his grandfather. I must say he looks a nice young man – with excellent manners."

Meg hobbled to the stairs, thinking about the evening. "I felt like a fine young lady, dancing and coming home by carriage."

"I don't believe real fine young ladies could have enjoyed themselves more than us, in spite of our burned hair, scorched gowns and only one good glove each," declared Jo, with a grin.

# Chapter 3
## Amy's crime

One morning, Meg came down to find Amy sobbing her heart out over the kitchen table.

"I'm dreadfully in debt," Amy wept.

"What do you mean?" asked Meg.

Amy sniffed. "I owe a dozen pickled limes at school. They're all the fashion. The girls keep buying them and I eat theirs, and now I must pay them back but I don't have any money."

"How much do you need?" said Meg, opening her purse.

"Oh thank you, Meg darling!" Amy cried.

"I'll buy them on the way to school." She didn't tell Meg that limes had been forbidden.

The news that Amy had limes soon spread. As the class began, a girl who disliked Amy shot up her hand. "Please sir, Amy March has limes in her desk!"

The teacher was furious. He made Amy throw the plump limes out of the window, one by one. Then he caned her hands in front of the entire class.

"You won't go back," their mother comforted Amy that night. "That school is full of spoiled, badly brought-up children. Still, it was your fault too. You did break the rules."

"I h-had t-to…" Amy couldn't stop crying. "It was so humiliating not having any pickled limes."

"I'll teach you at home instead," Jo offered later, picking up her hat as she spoke.

"Th-thank you," Amy gulped. "Where are you going, Jo?"

"To see a play with Laurie."

"Take me with you," begged Amy.

"No," said Jo firmly. "You're too young."

"Oh, please…" Amy wheedled.

"No."

"You'll be sorry, Jo March," Amy yelled at her.

"And I just offered to teach you!" Jo yelled back. "Spoiled brat," she added, slamming the door on her way out.

When Jo came back from the play, she started looking for her notebook. With panic in her voice, she asked if anyone had seen it. "Beth? Meg? Amy? Do you know where it is? The blue one, with all my stories in it?"

Everyone shook their heads, but Amy blushed a guilty red.

"Amy, you've got it!" cried Jo.

"No I haven't."

"You know where it is then."

"I burned it," Amy snapped.

"*Burned* it!"

The whole family knew how precious the book was. Jo had worked on it for months, hoping some of the stories might even be good enough to print.

Jo shook Amy, until her teeth chattered, crying passionately, "You wicked girl! I can never write those stories again! I'll never forgive you!"

Beth flew to comfort Jo while Meg scolded Amy.

"I feel dreadful," Amy said at bedtime. "Please forgive me Jo. I'm very, very sorry."

"I'll never forgive you," Jo repeated. "It was an abominable thing to do."

Amy turned away. "Now I wish I hadn't said sorry," she snapped. "And I'm not. So there!"

The next morning, Jo was still furious about her notebook. Wanting to get out of the house, she asked Laurie to go skating with her.

Amy watched them leave from her bedroom window. "Bother!" she thought.

"Jo promised to take me skating next time, but she's too cross. Well, I'll just go anyway!"

When Amy arrived, Jo and Laurie were already zig-zagging down the river.

"Keep to the side," Laurie called to Jo. "The ice is getting too thin in the middle." Amy, far behind, didn't hear.

Jo looked back and saw Amy coming after them. "She can take care of herself, mean pig," she thought, angrily.

Amy aimed straight for the middle, but Jo skated on, with a strange feeling inside her. There was a sudden scream and the terrible sound of cracking ice. Jo spun around. Amy had vanished. Only her hood could be seen, bobbing in the water.

"Grab a branch!" Laurie shouted. For a second, Jo stood frozen with terror, before she pulled herself together. She sped off and returned with a strong branch, to find Laurie lying on the ice, desperately clutching one of Amy's hands.

Jo thrust the far end of the branch into Amy's reach and helped to pull her, gasping and coughing, from the freezing water. Jo hugged Amy tight, swiftly taking off her dripping things and wrapping her warmly in her own dry clothes.

"Suppose she'd drowned!" Jo agonized, after she and their mother had tucked Amy into bed. "Sometimes I get so angry, I lose control. I wish I didn't."

"I used to be just like you," Mrs. March confided. "Don't worry, Jo. I still get angry too, but I try not to show it. If you keep trying, you'll conquer your anger."

Her mother's quiet sympathy and understanding helped Jo more than any scolding could have done.

# Chapter 4
# Party girl

That summer, Meg was invited to stay with her friend, Sallie Moffat.

"If only I didn't have to work..." she grumbled. Then, at the last minute, the children she looked after caught measles.

"I can go after all!" Meg realized excitedly.

Her sisters helped her to pack. "A whole week of fun!" Beth said, picking out hair ribbons for Meg to take.

Amy was green with envy. "Ooh, I wish I was going to a house party. You are lucky."

Jo began to fold Meg's skirts, looking like a windmill with her long arms. "What did Mother give you out of the treasure chest?" she wanted to know.

The treasure chest, made of sweet-smelling cedar wood, was where their mother kept her best things.

"A pretty fan, a blue sash and a pair of silk stockings," said Meg. "There was a length of violet silk, too, but there isn't time to have it made into a dress, even if Mother would let me, so I must be content with my old white cotton, I suppose." She sighed.

"Never mind, you always look lovely in white," Beth consoled her.

"I wish I hadn't smashed my coral bracelet. It would have suited you so," mourned Jo, who loved to lend her things – though they were usually too broken to be of much use.

"My white isn't low-necked and it doesn't rustle like a silk dress," Meg said crossly. "But it will have to do because there isn't anything else."

"You said the other day you'd be perfectly happy if you could only go to Sallie Moffat's," Beth reminded her.

Meg gave a rueful laugh. "So I did. I suppose the more you have the more you want."

Meg was overawed by the Moffats' stylish and enormous house. She loved eating their extravagant meals, riding in their carriages and dressing up every day to go shopping and to concerts and on elegant picnics.

Sallie Moffat's pretty things filled her with envy, and home soon seemed bare and dull by comparison.

The house was full of Sallie's friends, all girls the same age, but not one of them earned a living like Meg. She began to copy their airs and graces and to feel ill-used and overworked.

The highlight of the week was the Spring Ball. The girls spent their time chatting about which dresses to wear.

"I have a new pink silk," Sallie said.
"What are you wearing, Meg?"

"My old white," said Meg, blushing.

"Let's see," everyone begged.

As Meg displayed it there was a stunned
silence. Meg saw the other girls look at it, then
at one another. She felt her cheeks burn as
she thought how they must pity her. Waves of
bitterness swept over her as the others showed
off their beautiful ball dresses, which billowed
like clouds of gauzy butterflies.

"You can't wear the white. It's a day
dress," Sallie said at last. "I know!
We'll dress you up."

She called her French maid and
between them they transformed
Meg. They powdered her neck
and arms, rubbed her with scent,
rouged her cheeks, painted her lips
and crimped her hair.

296

Then they laced her into a blue silk dress so tight Meg gasped for breath. The dress left her shoulders bare and the front was cut low. Finally, they decked her out like a Christmas tree, with bracelets, brooch, necklace and earrings. They even tucked a silver butterfly in her hair.

"Beautiful!" said Sallie.

But something had fled out of Meg. Her simplicity and freshness had disappeared and in their place was a frilled fashion doll, no different from any of the other girls.

Meg felt strange, but excited, as she teetered downstairs to the ball in her borrowed, high-heeled, blue silk shoes.

"Don't trip!" giggled Sallie.

To her delight, Meg found that the fashionable guests in the house party, who had ignored her in her shabby clothes, now swarmed to her like bees to honey. She loved being so popular and drank glass after glass of champagne. She was flirting over her fan when she saw Laurie coming up to her.

"Meg! What have you done?"

Meg fluttered her eyelashes. "It's the new Meg! Don't you like her?"

"Not a bit," said Laurie gravely. "I don't like dressed-up girls. And what would Jo say if she saw you?"

Just then they heard people talking behind them.

"Mrs. March has laid her plans. She keeps trying to pair off one of her girls with the rich Laurence boy. Those Marches haven't a penny to their name. It would be a fine match for them. Look at that girl. She knows how to play her cards."

Meg went pale under her rouged cheeks. "How dare they! It's not true." She'd never felt so angry and ashamed.

"Don't listen, Meg. It's just silly gossip," Laurie whispered.

"Don't tell Mother and the girls about this," Meg begged Laurie. "I'd rather tell them myself."

"I won't," he promised. "But don't drink any more champagne," he added, in a brotherly way. "You'll have a splitting headache tomorrow."

Back at home, Meg told her mother everything. "I let them make a fool of me, and I flirted and behaved so badly. I just couldn't help myself – it's so nice to be praised and admired."

"Of course it is," said her mother, "but be careful your love of praise doesn't make you do silly things. Enjoy yourself, but be modest as well, Meg."

Blushing, Meg described the gossip she'd overheard. "Mother, do you have 'plans' for us?"

Mrs. March stroked her daughter's anxious face.

"Meg, my only plan is for you to marry for love. If you were happy, I wouldn't mind if you married a poor man or didn't ever marry."

"Sallie says a poor girl has no luck," Meg said.

"Sallie's wrong," said her mother firmly. "Be yourself, Meg, good and kind, and leave the rest to time."

Meg smiled at her mother. "Home may not be rich or splendid, but it's the best place in the world."

# Chapter 5
# Shocking news

When Laurie went on outings with the March girls, he often brought his tutor along. John Brooke was a thoughtful man, with friendly brown eyes and a gentle presence.

"Have you seen how Brooke looks at Meg?" Laurie asked Jo, one afternoon.

"Meg wouldn't dream of falling in love with him," snapped Jo. "She's tired of flirting and men. Come on, let's go to the post office. I want to see if there's a new story magazine out."

There was. Laurie and Jo brought it home. Jo flung herself down and read as if she were gobbling it up.

"Read it aloud," urged Meg. "We haven't heard a new story for ages."

"Brilliant!" was the general opinion when Jo finished.

"Who wrote it?" asked Amy.

With an odd mix of solemnity and excitement in her voice, Jo replied, "Your sister!"

Beth flung her arms around Jo. "Oh, you're so clever!"

"The magazine editor paid me for this one and he's asked me for more stories. I'll be able to help us all."

Mrs. March gazed at Jo fondly. "Your father would be so proud," she said.

A sharp ring at the door interrupted them. It was a telegraph boy bearing a telegram with the stark instruction:

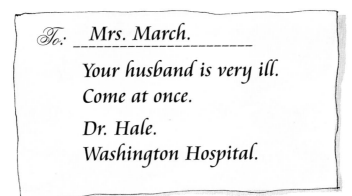

To: ___Mrs. March._____

**Your husband is very ill.
Come at once.**

**Dr. Hale.
Washington Hospital.**

Instantly, the whole world seemed to change, as the happy atmosphere collapsed around them. Mrs. March rose shakily to start packing. Laurie and Jo rushed from the house. Beth hugged her cat tightly while Amy simply stood still as a statue.

Laurie returned with John Brooke.

"Would your mother like me to escort her?" he asked Meg. "It's a difficult journey, and the war makes it even harder for women to travel alone."

Meg was full of gratitude. "That's so kind of you, John."

"Grandfather sent these to help the invalid," said Laurie, squeezing some bottles of brandy into their mother's luggage, along with a warm dressing gown, bandages and a blanket.

Jo raced in excitedly, her bonnet tied tightly under her chin, and handed a purse full of money to her mother.

"Aunt March sent this. She said Father was stupid to go to war when he was so old, she knew no good would come of it, and she hoped that you'd take her advice next time."

Mrs. March tightened her lips, and Jo guessed that she was trying to keep her temper. But her mother only said, "Take off your bonnet, Jo."

Jo pulled it off and a cry rose from her family. Her beautiful long chestnut hair had been cut as short as a boy's.

"What have you done?" gasped Amy.

"I sold it," Jo said proudly. "I saw tails of hair for sale in a barber's window, so I asked him to cut mine off to get more money for Father."

Mrs. March was overwhelmed. "Oh, Jo. You shouldn't have."

"Nonsense. It will do my brains good to have that mop taken off. Besides, it'll be boyish and easy to keep tidy."

Amy fingered her own ringlets. "How could you?" she asked.

"She doesn't look like Jo any more, but I love her for it," Beth said softly.

# Chapter 6
## Beth

Mrs. March left for Washington at once. A week later, they heard from Mr. Brooke that Father was recovering. The news made everyone feel happier. Meg and Jo worked hard at their jobs, Beth and Amy cleaned the house and they shared the cooking.

But, one by one, they slipped back into their old ways. Meg spent hours reading John Brooke's letters. Jo curled up with her writing and Amy went back to sketching.

Only Beth faithfully carried out their mother's
duties, taking food to families in the poorer
part of town. One afternoon, she was drenched
in a downpour of winter sleet. When she got
home, the fire was out and she couldn't get
warm. A few days later, Beth started shivering
as though she'd never stop. At the same time,
she felt boiling hot. Jo found her looking in the
medicine cupboard.

"I don't feel well," Beth muttered, going
to press her burning head against the cold
window pane.

Jo felt Beth's forehead and was horrified. "Beth, you're feverish. We must get the doctor."

When the doctor came, he looked serious. "The child has scarlet fever," he announced and sent her straight to bed.

Beth grew worse and worse. Amy was sent to stay with Aunt March to keep her out of the way and Meg continued to work though both of them longed to be at home. Jo spent all her time nursing her sister. Beth never complained, but sometimes when the fever was very bad, she didn't seem to recognize Jo, and would cry out for their mother.

Snow fell. It lay in drifts around the garden, as white as Beth's face. During the restless, anxious hours in Beth's room, Jo realized how much she loved her.

Beth's shyness meant she was the quietest of the sisters, but her kindness and gentleness made her all the more precious. All of them had ambitions except Beth. Meg wanted to marry, Jo was determined to be an author and Amy dreamed of being an artist. Beth just wanted to make people happy.

One afternoon, Laurie caught Jo having a private cry.

"I wish I didn't have a heart, it aches so," she sobbed.

Laurie's eyes were wet too as he comforted her. "We mustn't give up hope. That won't help Beth. I've sent a telegram to your mother," he added. "I think she should come home."

Their mother came as soon as she could, brightness and courage shining from her. That night Beth's fever broke. The doctor confirmed it. "She's still weak," he said, "but I think she'll pull through."

315

## Chapter 7
# Endings and beginnings

Like sunshine after a storm, several peaceful weeks followed. In Washington, Mr. March was getting stronger every day and Beth was soon well enough to come downstairs and lie on the study sofa.

Christmas Day dawned mild and sunny. Laurie ran in and out with presents and Jo made ridiculous speeches as she presented each one.

"I'm so full of happiness, that if only Father were here I couldn't hold one more drop," sighed Beth.

"So am I," agreed Jo, gloating over one of her presents, a brand-new novel.

"And me," echoed Amy, looking at a delicate framed print from her mother.

"I know I am!" said Meg, admiring the silvery folds of her first silk dress – a gift from old Mr. Laurence.

Laurie looked so excited he could hardly contain himself. "Here's another present for the March family!" he cried.

And there stood a tall man, muffled up to the eyebrows, supported by Mr. Brooke. "Father!" the girls cried. In an instant, the house was in uproar. Mrs. March was half-laughing, half-crying, Jo almost fainted and Amy fell on her father's feet and hugged his boots.

When they had recovered themselves, Mr. March was settled in an easy chair, Beth on his lap, and Christmas dinner was served. The fat turkey was browned to perfection and the plum pudding melted in their mouths.

Old Mr. Laurence and Laurie joined them, along with John Brooke, who kept sneaking admiring glances at Meg. She blushed and smiled back. Jo spent most of the meal glowering at the unfortunate tutor, much to Laurie's amusement.

They ate and drank and talked and laughed. The day ended with Beth playing carols and everyone singing.

The following afternoon, Aunt March arrived to visit her nephew and surprised John Brooke and Meg talking quietly together. "Bless me, what's this?" she cried, looking from the pale young man to her blushing niece.

"This is Laurie's tutor and Father's friend," stammered Meg. John nodded shyly, and vanished into the study.

"He's not thinking of proposing I hope?" boomed the old lady. "He's not nearly good enough for you."

"Why not?" Meg demanded.

Aunt March sniffed. "He's a poor wretch and probably after the money he thinks I'm leaving you in my will."

Meg was so indignant that her voice soared louder than Aunt March's. "John's not like that! He's good and kind, which matters more than riches."

In the study, John heard every word. His heart swelled with happiness. "Perhaps Meg will marry me even though I don't have any money," he thought.

321

"Highty tighty!" said Aunt March. "Is that the way you take my advice, young lady? You'll soon tire of love in a cottage."

"I don't mind being poor," Meg replied firmly. "John and I work hard. We'll earn our way and be proud of it."

As Aunt March stormed off in a huff, John raced from the study and took Meg in his arms. Not long after, Jo entered the drawing room to see her sister sitting on John's lap.

Meg jumped up but John smiled. "Congratulate us, Jo. We're engaged."

Appalled at the thought of losing Meg, Jo raced upstairs and begged her parents to do something. But Mr. and Mrs. March were thrilled at the news and so were Amy and Beth. Even Laurie dashed around with an enormous bunch of flowers for them as soon as he heard.

"What a year this has been," said Mrs. March, "but it's ended well."

"Hmm," murmured Jo, not liking the thought of her family breaking up.

Laurie nudged her. "Cheer up," he said. "You'll always have me."

Jo grinned.

"Don't you wish we could see into the future?" Laurie asked.

"No," said Jo, looking at her family. "I might see something sad and I don't believe any of us could be happier than we are this very minute."

# Heidi

# Johanna Spyri (1827-1901)

Johanna Spyri, a doctor's daughter, was
born in the Swiss countryside
and grew up loving the mountains. Her
first book, *A Leaf on Vrony's Grave*
was published in 1871, and
was followed by many
stories for both adults
and children.
*Heidi* was published
nine years later. It was
an instant success,
and remains as
popular as
ever today.

# Chapter 1
## Meeting Grandfather

Heidi felt cross and tired as Aunt Dete pulled
her up the steep slope.

"I'd go faster if I wasn't wearing *all* my
clothes," said Heidi.

"You'll need them at your grandfather's and I don't want to carry them," said her aunt, angrily.

"Do you think Grandfather will want me?" Heidi asked nervously.

Aunt Dete shook her head. "I don't know. He's a miserable old man and he hasn't seen you since you were a baby. But I've taken care of you for long enough. Now it's his turn."

At last they reached
Grandfather's hut, at the
very top of the mountain.
Dete rapped sharply on
the door. It creaked
open and an old
man peered out.

"What do you want?"
he asked, gruffly.

329

"This is your granddaughter, Heidi," Dete explained. "Your dead son's child. I've brought her to live with you."

"Take her away," said the old man, trying to shut the door. "I don't want her."

"I don't care," Dete snapped. "You have to take her. Both her parents are dead. I've found a good job in Frankfurt and she can't come with me."

With that,
Heidi's aunt turned
and ran down the mountain.

331

Grandfather stared silently at Heidi.
Heidi stared back.

"He doesn't want me," she thought, sadly,
"but where else can I go?"

"Well... you'd better come in," said
Grandfather, with a scowl.

Heidi stepped into the hut and looked
around. There didn't seem to be room for
her anywhere.

"Where shall I sleep?"
she asked. Grandfather shrugged. He didn't
even look at her. "You'll have to find your own
bed," he growled.

Heidi looked again and saw a ladder in the corner. Feeling curious, she climbed up into a hayloft. From the window, she could see a green valley far below and hear pine trees whooshing in the wind.

She lifted some of the sweet-smelling hay, puffing it up into the shape of a mattress. "I'll sleep here," she called. "It's lovely!"

"She shows some sense," Grandfather muttered to himself. "Come down now," he ordered. "It's time for supper."

335

Heidi watched Grandfather blow onto the embers of the fire, making the flames blaze. Bringing a bowl, he filled it to the brim with rich, creamy milk.

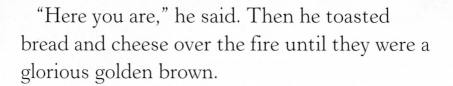

"Here you are," he said. Then he toasted bread and cheese over the fire until they were a glorious golden brown.

Delicious smells filled the hut and Heidi realized how hungry she was. She licked up oozing drips of cheese, crunched the toast and drank the milk to the last drop.

Through the open door, she saw the sky and mountainside glow in the setting sun. "I like it here, Grandfather," she said.

337

That night, Heidi snuggled down in the hayloft.
As she fell asleep she wondered why Grandfather
lived all alone, high on the mountain. What had
happened to make him so sad and unfriendly?

# Chapter 2
# The goat boy

Early next morning, Heidi woke to the sound of bells. She sat up. Sunshine poured through the hayloft window, turning her straw bed into shimmering gold.

Quickly, she dressed and shot down the ladder. A boy was standing at the door, whistling.

"This is Peter, the goat boy," Grandfather told her. "He's come for Little Swan and Little Bear."

Two goats – one white, one brown – pushed past him and sniffed Heidi. She giggled as they licked her hands.

"Their tongues tickle!" she said.

"Do you want to come with me?" Peter shouted over the bleats and bells. "I'm going up the mountain to find fresh grass for them."

"Can I?" Heidi asked Grandfather.

"I suppose," he replied. "But have your breakfast first." He sat on a stool and milked Little Bear, then handed Heidi a bowl of fresh milk.

"Come on!" said Peter, as soon as she'd finished. "You can stay at the back and make sure none of the goats get lost."

As they ran over rocks to the mountain pastures, Peter showed Heidi all the mountain's secrets.

He pointed to an eagle's nest hidden in the craggy peaks and the spots where wild flowers grew. The mountain looked as if a giant had scattered handfuls of jewels over it.

Heidi had never seen so many flowers. She picked great blue and yellow bunches for Grandfather.

Every day, Heidi went out with Peter and the goats. And every day, her cheeks grew rosier and her eyes more sparkly. Grandfather fed her crusty bread, tasty cheese and Little Swan's milk. At night, he told her stories by the fire.

Heidi had never been happier... until one morning, when the door flew open and there stood Aunt Dete in a brand new dress.

"I've come for Heidi," she announced. "I should never have left her with you in the first place."

"No," cried Heidi, suddenly afraid. "I like it here. I want to stay with Grandfather."

Dete ignored her. "I've found a place for Heidi in Frankfurt," she told Grandfather. "Clara Sesemann, a little girl who's always ill, wants a friend to keep her company."

"If Heidi behaves," her aunt went on, "Mr. Sesemann will pay her and buy her some fine new clothes. It's a great chance for her."

Grandfather had been looking crosser and crosser during this speech. "Take her and spoil her then!" he bellowed at Dete. "But don't bother coming back. Ever!"

Ignoring Heidi's protests, Dete gripped her arm and dragged her outside. As they left, Heidi saw Grandfather sitting alone, his head in his hands.

"Poor Grandfather!" cried Heidi, tears trickling down her face.

"Come *on*, Heidi," said Dete, pushing her down the mountain. "I'm sorry I ever left you with that sad old man."

"Why is he so sad?" asked Heidi.

"He thinks the world is a bad place," her aunt replied. "First, his wife died. Then your father, his only child, wasted all his money and died too. But your grandfather's just made things worse for himself."

"He said there was only misery in the world and shut himself away up here. Forget him, Heidi. Think about Frankfurt."

"I'll never forget him!" cried Heidi.

"It's for your own good," Dete declared, striding off.

Heidi was quiet, but secretly she made a promise. "One day I'll come back to him."

# Chapter 3
## Heidi and Clara

It was a long journey to Frankfurt. The sun was beginning to set when they stopped before a grand house in a cobbled street.

Dete pulled the bell. "This is it," she muttered.

A well-dressed servant opened the door and led them into a vast hall.

Heidi felt very small and shabby. She felt even worse when the housekeeper, Mrs. Rotenmeyer, saw her.

"You look most unsuitable," she said to Heidi with a sigh. "I suppose you'd better meet Clara."

Clara lay on a heap of pillows in a frilly four-poster bed. Her face was pale and the room was hot.

"Thank you for coming, Heidi," she said, quietly. "I'll like having company. I can't get out of bed."

"Why not?" asked Heidi.

"I've been sick and I'm still weak," Clara explained. "I don't think I'll ever get better."

"No one could get better in this hot, stuffy room," Heidi thought. She ran over to a window and flung it wide open.

The street below jostled with people, horses and carriages. Heidi could hear strange music mixed in with the clattering hooves and footsteps.

Leaning out, she saw a ragged boy with a street organ. A pair of kittens peeked out of his pockets.

Heidi rushed downstairs and onto the street. "Can you come here?" she called, beckoning him over. "There's someone I want you to play for."

Moments later, they were both bounding up the stairs.

"Surprise!" shouted Heidi, throwing open Clara's door and letting in the ragged boy.

Downstairs, Mrs. Rotenmeyer the housekeeper was puzzled. She could hear singing, laughing, music, even kittens – and all coming from Clara's bedroom.

"What's going on in here?" she shrieked, as she stormed into Clara's room.

"How did this dreadful boy get in?" she demanded. "I blame you," she said, glaring at Heidi. "I knew you were trouble from the moment I saw you. Go to your room at once."

"No," pleaded Clara. "Heidi was only trying to cheer me up." She held Heidi's hand. "Please don't send Heidi to her room. We want to have our supper together."

There was nothing Mrs. Rotenmeyer could do. She had to obey Clara. "All right," she said crossly, turning to go, "but get that dirty boy out of here now!"

Mrs. Rotenmeyer returned carrying a tray loaded with rich food. Greasy chunks of meat swam in a cream sauce. Clara pushed it around her plate and hardly ate anything. Heidi didn't like it either.

"I don't get hungry lying in bed," Clara murmured.

"You'd soon get hungry running up the mountain to Grandfather's hut," Heidi told her.

Clara looked sad. "But since I've been ill, I can't walk."

"That's terrible," said Heidi.

The warm room and heavy meal were making her feel sleepy. She had to go outside to breathe some fresh air.

Stale smells hung over the noisy, dirty, street. Heidi longed for the cool clear air of the mountain and the soft breeze that made the pine trees rustle.

Some time after Heidi's arrival, the servants started claiming the house was haunted by a ghost.

"A white figure floats down the stairs at night," said a maid.

The servants were so upset, Mrs. Rotenmeyer grew worried. "I must tell Clara's father," she decided.

Mr. Sesemann only laughed when Mrs. Rotenmeyer told him about the servants' fears. "There's no such thing as ghosts," he said. "I'll catch your ghost to prove it."

The next night he waited in the hall at the bottom of the stairs. Heidi came down, wearing a white nightgown. She tried to open the locked front door, then sobbed.

Mr. Sesemann went over to her and saw she was still fast asleep.

"Heidi has been sleepwalking," Mr. Sesemann explained to Clara and Mrs. Rotenmeyer, the next morning. "The poor child is so homesick, I think she'd better go home."

Clara looked sad. "I'll miss you, Heidi," she said.

# Chapter 4
# Heidi goes home

The following week, Grandfather looked out of the window and could hardly believe his eyes. A peculiar procession was stumbling up the mountain slope.

Two men were struggling with suitcases. A third hauled a wheelchair and a fourth carried a child bundled up in a shawl. The men puffed and panted, their shirts drenched in sweat.

Ahead of them all danced Heidi.

She raced up the slope and threw herself into Grandfather's arms.

"Heidi!" he cried. "You've come back to me. I thought I'd never see you again."

"I missed you," Heidi said. "Look, Mr. Sesemann has written you a letter to explain."

*Dear Sir,*

*Heidi was too homesick to stay with us but Clara could not bear to say goodbye. I hope you will forgive me for sending her with Heidi to stay for a month.*

*Clara, alas, is still very weak after a long illness. She has no appetite and cannot walk. I hope her visit to you on the mountain will give her new strength.*

*With all my thanks and best wishes,*

*Yours sincerely,*

**Hans Sesemann**

Grandfather turned to Clara.

"I'm very pleased to meet you," he said. "And thank you for bringing Heidi back to me. You'll soon feel better breathing our mountain air."

Grandfather put Clara's wheelchair in the sunshine, so she could see the wonderful view, and gave her a bowl of fresh milk.

"Guess who really gave you the milk?" Heidi teased, bringing Little Swan over. The goat butted Clara gently, until she realized Little Swan wanted to be stroked.

Clara drank thirstily. "This tastes much nicer than Frankfurt milk," she said.

"Heidi?" came a shout. Peter ran up the path to them. "I heard you were back," he said to Heidi.

"Come out with me tomorrow," he urged her.

"Peter, I can't," said Heidi. "I have to stay with Clara."

Peter gave Clara a jealous look.

"You go Heidi," Clara insisted. "I'll be fine."

All the same, when they set off next morning, Clara looked sad.

"I'll be quick," Heidi promised. "I just want to climb the ridge where the biggest, bluest flowers grow."

Clara watched them go longingly. She would have given anything to be running with them, with strong legs that could skip and jump.

"I wish you'd come," Heidi told Clara when she returned. "We watched an eagle soar above our heads and did somersaults down the mountain."

Clara sighed. "Oh I wish I could walk!"

"Cheer up," said Grandfather. "The sun has already brought roses to your cheeks. I'm sure you'll soon feel stronger."

"And I won't leave you again," Heidi promised.

From where he stood, high on the mountain, Peter could see Heidi and Clara talking together. His heart burned with jealousy.

"I wish that girl hadn't come," he thought. "Heidi's *my* friend. I'll *make* Clara go home." And a plan began to form in his mind.

# Chapter 5
# Peter's plan

Before sunrise next morning, Peter crept to Grandfather's hut. All was quiet and still.

Just as Peter hoped, Clara's wheelchair stood by the door. Noiselessly, he pushed it to the edge of the mountain and rolled it over a steep, stony cliff.

The chair hit the rocks with a terrible clatter.
An endless echo followed its fall, BANG...
CLANG... again and again.

Peering over the cliff, Peter saw the jagged
rocks had smashed the wheelchair into
a thousand pieces. Peter looked
at what he had done...
and fled.

When he arrived at the hut for the
goats, Heidi told Peter about
Clara's chair. "The wind must
have caught it," she said.

"Grandfather has to carry Clara everywhere."

"Then Clara will have to go home, won't she?"
Peter demanded.

"Aha," murmured Grandfather. "I think I
know who blew that puff of wind."

Heidi was shocked. "Did you do it, Peter?" she asked, sharply.

Peter went red. "I'm... I'm sorry," he stammered. "I wanted her to go. You don't have time for me now."

"Peter, you must hate me," said Clara. "You think I've taken Heidi away from you."

"Never mind," Heidi interrupted. "We can all still be friends."

But Grandfather shook his head.

"Mr. Sesemann may not be so forgiving," he said. "Clara's chair is still broken."

"If only Clara could walk..." said Heidi.
"I do feel stronger," Clara whispered.
"Perhaps I could try."

She edged herself forward and put her slender feet on the ground. Grandfather gently took hold of her hands and helped her to stand.

"My legs feel so weak," said Clara, trembling.

"Be brave," said Grandfather.

Slowly, Clara put one foot in front of the other.

Clara wobbled, but Grandfather supported her.

"Rest now," he ordered. "You can try again tomorrow."

Every day, Clara walked a little more. Hungry from the exercise and fresh mountain air, she wolfed down huge meals. Strength flowed into her and she tingled with energy. "Won't Father be amazed?" she thought.

# Chapter 6

# A surprise for Mr. Sesemann

A few weeks later, Mr. Sesemann arrived for Clara. He hardly recognized his daughter with her glowing face, bright eyes and thick, shiny hair.

379

When Clara stood up, he was astonished and when she walked up to him, he had to sit down.

"Is it really you?" he said. "I can't believe it. You're walking!"

"Isn't it wonderful," laughed Clara. "Grandfather and Heidi made it happen."

"And Peter," Grandfather put in, his eyes twinkling.

"You did it, Clara," said Heidi. "It was your hard work."

"It's a miracle," Mr. Sesemann beamed. "Clara, I'm proud of you. Thank you, thank you everyone."

"You must come back to the mountain whenever you want," Heidi told Clara.

"And you must come to Frankfurt – Peter too," said Clara. "We'll find the ragged boy again and dance."

When Clara and her father had gone, Heidi and Grandfather went outside to watch the sunset. The sky and mountains shone red-gold, just like Heidi's first evening.

"It's beautiful," said Grandfather.

"Once I was sad and lonely," he told Heidi, "but you've made me a happy man."

*Edited by Rachel Firth and Lesley Sims*

*Designed by Caroline Spatz*

*Additional design by Emily Bornoff*

*Cover Design: Zoe Wray*

This edition first published in 2014 by Usborne Publishing Ltd,
83-85 Saffron Hill, London EC1N 8RT, England.
www.usborne.com Copyright © 2014, 2008 Usborne Publishing Ltd.
The name Usborne and the devices ⚲ 🎈 are Trade Marks of Usborne
Publishing Ltd. All rights reserved. No part of this publication may be
reproduced, stored in a retrieval system, or transmitted in any form or by any
means, electronic, mechanical, photocopying, recording or otherwise,
without the prior permission of the publisher.
First published in America in 2009. UE.